SUPERCROSS and ARENA CROSS

Taking MX Indoors

Darren Sechrist

x1000r/min

CRABTREE PUBLISHING COMPANY
www.crabtreebooks.com

Crabtree Publishing Company

www.crabtreebooks.com

Coordinating editor: Chester Fisher
Series and project editor: Shoreline Publishing Group LLC
Author: Darren Sechrist
Series Consultant: Bryan Stealey
Project Manager: Kavita Lad
Art direction: Rahul Dhiman
Design: Ranjan Singh
Cover Design: Ranjan Singh
Photo research: Akansha Srivastava
Editors: Adrianna Morganelli, Mike Hodge

Acknowledgments

The publishers would like to thanks the following for permission
to reproduce photographs:

p4: Simon Cudby (top); p4: Paul Buckley (bottom); p5: Racer X Archive;
p6: ASSOCIATED PRESS; p7: Terry Good Collection; p8: Randy Petree;
p9: Matt Ware; p10: Simon Cudby; p11: Paul Buckley (all);
p12: Simon Cudby; p13: Simon Cudby (all); p14: Simon Cudby;
p15: Simon Cudby (all); p16: Simon Cudby; p17: Paul Buckley (top);
p17: Simon Cudby (bottom); p18: Simon Cudby; p19: Simon Cudby (all);
p20: Simon Cudby; p21: Simon Cudby (top); p21: Paul Buckley (bottom);
p22: Paul Buckley; p23: Paul Buckley (top); p23: Simon Cudby (bottom);
p24: Simon Cudby; p25: Simon Cudby (all); p26: Simon Cudby;
p27: Simon Cudby (left); p27: Paul Buckley (right); p28: Simon Cudby;
p29: Simon Cudby (top); p29: Matt Ware (bottom); p30: Simon Cudby;
p31: Paul Buckley (top); p31: Simon Cudby (bottom)

Cover and title page image provided by Steve Bruhn

Library and Archives Canada Cataloguing in Publication

Sechrist, Darren
    Supercross and arenacross / Darren Sechrist.

(MXplosion!)
Includes index.
ISBN 978-0-7787-3991-3 (bound).
--ISBN 978-0-7787-4004-9 (pbk.)

    1. Supercross--Juvenile literature. I. Title. II. Series.

GV1060.1455.S42 2008   j796.7'56   C2008-901220-8

Library of Congress Cataloging-in-Publication Data

Sechrist, Darren.
    Supercross and arenacross / Darren Sechrist.
        p. cm. -- (MXplosion!)
    Includes index.
    ISBN-13: 978-0-7787-4004-9 (pbk. : alk. paper)
    ISBN-10: 0-7787-4004-8 (pbk. : alk. paper)
    ISBN-13: 978-0-7787-3991-3 (reinforced library binding : alk. paper)
    ISBN-10: 0-7787-3991-0 (reinforced library binding : alk. paper)
    1. Supercross--Juvenile literature. I. Title. II. Series.

GV1060.1455.S43 2008
796.7'56--dc22

                                                                    2008006381

Crabtree Publishing Company

www.crabtreebooks.com   1-800-387-7650

Published in Canada
Crabtree Publishing
616 Welland Ave.
St. Catharines, ON
L2M 5V6

Published in the United States
Crabtree Publishing
PMB16A
350 Fifth Ave., Suite 3308
New York, NY 10118

Published in the United Kingdom
Crabtree Publishing
White Cross Mills
High Town, Lancaster
LA1 4XS

Published in Australia
Crabtree Publishing
386 Mt. Alexander Rd.
Ascot Vale (Melbourne)
VIC 3032

Contents

The World of Supercross

Supercross is one of the most popular motor sports today. The speed, the high-flying tricks, and the tight competition draw fans to stadiums across the United States. This exciting sport can trace its roots back to very modest beginnings almost 100 years ago.

The Birth of Motocross

Almost since motorcycles were invented, racing them has been popular. The sport was especially big in England, where many people used motorcycles for transportation. Organized racing dates back to the early 1900s in Yorkshire, England. Those early events were more like skills competitions—speed was not even a category in the judging! The 1924 Southern Scott Scramble is believed to be the first major outdoor motorcycle race like the ones that we know today. Today, outdoor motorcycle racing on dirt tracks is known as motocross, or MX for short.

Thanks to bumps and hills on the courses, riders like Chad Reed spend time in the air as well as in the dirt.

Riders like superstar Jeremy McGrath wear helmets, boots, gloves, goggles, and heavy-duty chest and arm guards.

Zooming Beyond England

By the 1940s, the sport started to take off outside of England. The first Motocross des Nations event was held in Holland in 1947. It drew riders from Great Britain, Holland, and Belgium. The competition was a big hit and became an annual event. At the same time, Americans were starting to hold their own motorcycle races. One of the earliest events was the TT (tourist trophy), held by New York's Crotona Motorcycle Club in the 1920s. Over the next several decades, these events started popping up across the country. Many early races were **grassroots** events, loosely organized by racers and run on outdoor courses.

Heating Up: The 1950s and 1960s

By the 1950s and 1960s, the sport really started to catch on in America. Lighter, more **agile** bikes made the races more exciting. European riders, such as Torsten Hallman, began invading the United States to compete in these races. They brought a new, daring style that allowed them to win competitions and thrill U.S. fans. U.S. riders took note and quickly caught up to their European competition. U.S. riders were soon world-class and began drawing more attention from fans and the **media**. Today, motocross racing continues to grow, especially in America. But the way that most fans enjoy their racing isn't in the mud of the outdoors, but from the comfort of stadium seats. Supercross, or SX, is the indoor version of motocross. SX races are held in stadiums and draw tens of thousands of fans to each event. Have a seat, and let's follow the rapid rise of this cool way to enjoy motocross racing.

MX races started outdoors on courses carved out of hills or large, empty lots. Well-protected riders, like Kent Howerton here, circled the courses several times in a race.

5

MX Moves Indoors

Although supercross has risen to great heights in the United States, Americans were not the first ones to try stadium racing. Earlier attempts were made in Europe.

France and Czechoslovakia

On August 28, 1948, fans poured into Buffalo Stadium in Montrouge, France. They had come to see a brand new type of event. Other motorcycle races had been held at the stadium, but this race was different. This one would be more like an outdoor race: riders would have to contend with jumps, a water hazard, and other challenges. It was the first race that was anything like the supercross events that we see today. In 1956, Czechoslovakia (a country that has since split in two—the Czech Republic and Slovakia) got into the act. A dirt course was built at Strahov Stadium, and top riders from the region participated. More than 100,000 fans showed up to see racers speed around a half-mile course. Wooden ramps covered in dirt provided jumps for the riders. Both the Czech and French events were successful, but neither caught on enough to be a yearly event.

Supercross Comes to America

In the United States, outdoor motorcycle racing had been around since the 1930s, but indoor motorcycle racing didn't start until the 1960s. The earliest known event was a race at Miami Stadium in 1961. Ascot Speedway in Gardena, California (near Los Angeles), also hosted

Riders like "Hurricane" Bob Hannah (above) helped jump-start the sport of motocross in the United States, attracting new fans to this European import.

6

Dirty from the start: here's action from a 1956 race in Czechoslovakia.

weekly races in 1968, but the sport as it is known today got its real start in the early 1970s. In 1971, **promoters** set up an MX race on the infield at Florida's Daytona International Speedway. Daytona is usually the home of **NASCAR**'s biggest stock-car race, the Daytona 500. Motor-sports fans were used to heading to the gigantic **tri-oval** track to watch cars race, but in the 1971 event, they filled the infield at the center of the track to watch high-flying two-wheeled action. The popularity of this close-up form of motocross racing spread quickly. Fans liked what they saw of supercross and were ready for more.

The Super Bowl!

At this point in the story, Michael Goodwin came into the sport. Goodwin was a concert promoter who had fallen in love with motocross. He decided to stage his own race inside the Los Angeles Coliseum in California. He wanted his race to be the biggest event in the sport—like a "Super Bowl of Motocross." The race was held on July 8, 1972. Top riders from Europe and America competed, and 16-year-old American Marty Tripes won. Some 28,000 fans attended the race, and 38,000 showed up for a repeat of the race the following year. The name was soon shortened to "supercross," and a new, truly American sport was born.

Growing by Leaps and Bounds

Kick-started by the Super Bowl of Motocross, indoor racing action heated up in the 1970s, with new stars bringing more and more fans into stadiums and arenas.

AMA Shows the Way

Moving motocross into large stadiums brought a whole new audience to SX. Michael Goodwin had heavily advertised his early events on radio and television. People who might not know all that much about motorcycles or racing were now hearing about this new sport. Many of them decided to go see what all the fuss was about. At the races, they got to see top riders pushing themselves and their bikes to the limit. The high-speed action and the acrobatics hooked in a whole new group of fans. After the early success of Goodwin's "Super Bowl" events, similar races were soon being held across the country. The American Motorcyclist Association (AMA) organized a supercross racing series in 1974. The group held events at venues across the country. Riders would compete at these races and earn points toward the yearly AMA championship.

Archrivals Marty Smith (9) and Bob Hannah (5) duel in a 1977 Trans-AMA race.

From silence to roaring engines! At the start of an arenacross race, the bikes leap into action as the starting gate is dropped.

Here Comes the Hurricane

The late 1970s saw the entry of the first big star of supercross, "Hurricane" Bob Hannah. Hannah grew up in Lancaster, California, where he learned about motorcycles from his father. He started out his racing career competing in local motocross events. Hannah tried racing in AMA Supercross in 1977. He was an immediate success, winning six of 10 races and his first AMA championship. He won the next two championships as well. When he retired in 1987, he had won 27 AMA supercross events—the most by any rider at that time. Supercross continued to grow steadily in popularity. The AMA tour added new stops, and fans filled up the stadiums to see the races.

Arenacross: Supercross on a Small Scale

Not every city has a large stadium where fans can see supercross. As SX grew in popularity during the 1980s, organizers started looking for ways to bring the speed and excitement of SX to more fans. They decided to try staging races in hockey arenas, basketball stadiums, and civic centers. The fans didn't seem to mind the cozier tracks and were soon flocking to the races. The new sport was called "arenacross," and it quickly became quite popular.

SX Goes Big Time

By the 1990s, the sport was ready to explode in popularity. Often a sport needs a "face" to really attract attention. Supercross had not one, but two, and these back-to-back superstars helped SX grow even bigger.

Two SX Heroes

During the 1990s and 2000s, supercross rose to new heights for several reasons. Probably the biggest reasons for this surge were two of the sport's most talented riders. Jeremy McGrath (also known as the "King of Supercross") arrived on the scene in the early 1990s and immediately became the sport's biggest star. Ricky Carmichael followed soon afterward and provided McGrath with a worthy opponent on the track. The rivalry between these riders helped raise the level of competition in the sport—and boosted fan interest, too.

The 2000s Bring a Big Boost

Soon, supercross was bringing in fans in droves. By the early 2000s, supercross events were drawing a total of 700,000 fans to its events each year. By 2005, that number had more than doubled to 1.5 million! Television brought these races into the living rooms of millions of fans who might never consider attending a supercross event. Meanwhile, MTV's X Games were pumping up the popularity of "extreme sports" with teens across the country. The X Games featured lots of action sports, from skateboarding and in-line skating to some amazing, high-flying motorcycle-stunt events. Although McGrath and Carmichael have retired (though both sometimes come back for **exhibitions**), a host of other exciting riders have come along to light up supercross events. James Stewart Jr. and Chad Reed are among the stars that have helped keep supercross growing in popularity from coast to coast. As a result of the popularity of supercross, the number and type of racing events have grown, as well. There are now 17 stops in the AMA Supercross series. There are also independent events both overseas and here in the United States.

We love you, Ricky! The big smile and incredible talent of Ricky Carmichael put him head-and-shoulders above other riders, and No. 1 in the hearts of fans.

In the Pits

Supercross-event organizers go all-out to make sure fans have a great time. At most events, they make the **pit area** open to fans. The pit is where race teams work on the motorcycles and where riders hang out and meet with fans between races. SX riders know that the fans are their biggest supporters. They're usually very happy to meet fans, sign autographs, and get their pictures taken. Fans can also come away with cool free stuff that companies give out in the pit area. If you go to an SX event, get there early enough to take advantage of this cool "behind the scenes" deal.

The Classes of Supercross

The AMA has two classes of racing, separated by the type and power of the motorcycles they use: Supercross (formerly 250cc) and Lites (formerly 125cc). The Supercross class uses the most powerful motorcycles. It is sort of like the "Major Leagues" of motocross. The sport's top stars all race in the same class, and it is considered the highlight of the show. The Lites class uses smaller, more nimble bikes in its races. Almost every rider starts out in Lites before moving to the Supercross class.

A Lites motorcycle (top) differs from the Supercross bike (bottom) in the size and power of its engine. The controls and general style of both are similar.

Jeremy McGrath— It's Showtime!

Many fans call record-setting racer Jeremy McGrath the "King of Supercross." Others simply call him "Showtime." Whatever name you choose, there's no denying that he's been one of the most dominant stars in the sport.

BMX Boyhood

McGrath was born on November 19, 1971, and he grew up in southern California. While most supercross racers get started racing motorcycles early in their lives, McGrath took a different route. He started out competing in **BMX** (bicycle motocross) races. BMX racers speed around dirt tracks, making leaps and rattling over bumps, all while pedaling their bikes furiously. In BMX races, McGrath learned to ride competitively. He also learned the "Nac-Nac," a trick that he would later bring to supercross (see page 26).

Breaking into SX

By the time he was a teenager, McGrath was looking for a new challenge, and decided to give motorcycle racing a try. His father found a small motorcycle in a friend's garage, and McGrath had his first bike. For three years, he competed in the **amateur** ranks of motocross. At age 17, McGrath decided to join the pro ranks of supercross. He started out in the Lites division and was an instant success. In the three years between 1990 and 1992, he racked up 13 wins. If that sounds like a lot, it is. That impressive total was more than any rider who came before him!

The amazing Jeremy McGrath shows off the high-flying form that helped him win dozens of championships—and millions of fans around the world.

A Superstar in Supercross

But McGrath really made a name for himself when he moved to the Supercross class in 1993. There, he used a combination of great riding skills, blazing speed, and supreme confidence to win the Supercross-class championship. He was the first top-level rookie to ever accomplish this feat! McGrath never looked back. He won 72 Supercross-class events and seven AMA Supercross Championships before retiring from full-time riding in 2002. Those numbers put him 26 wins and two championships ahead of the next rider, Ricky Carmichael. Aside from McGrath's domination of supercross, he's also got a friendly personality that makes him a fan magnet. This combination helped raise the sport's popularity to new heights during the 1990s and early 2000s. His list of accomplishments also includes writing a 2005 book about his life in racing and organizing the Jeremy McGrath Invitational in October 2006. That event drew some of the top MX riders in the world.

After more than 70 Supercross races like this one, McGrath found himself accepting the trophy and then taking time to talk to his fans about how he'd won yet another title!

The Hero Is a G.O.A.T.

Although Jeremy McGrath was undoubtedly the biggest star in supercross, Ricky Carmichael was certainly a close second. Carmichael's success at every level of racing even earned him the nickname G.O.A.T."

Motocross Master

Motorcycles were a part of Carmichael's life right from the beginning. Born on November 27, 1979, he started riding when he was only three years old! Carmichael spent much of his childhood practicing on his family's private track with his cousins. The practice paid off when he started entering amateur events. There, he set many records before moving to the professional MX ranks in 1996. Carmichael's ferocious, all-out style was an immediate success at motocross events, as well. In fact, he was as dominant in AMA Motocross as he had been in the amateurs. From 1997 to 1999, he won three straight 125 National Motocross Championships. In 1997 and 1998, Carmichael made his mark in the Lites division of SX. Like everything else before it, the Lites seemed to come easily to Carmichael. He won 12 events in just two years, including every race in the 1998 Lites East series.

Knocking Off the King

By 1999, Carmichael had dominated every level of racing except for the Supercross class. That year, he decided to face that final challenge head-on, but the switch to the bigger bikes was not a smooth one.

One hand on the handlebars, one hand off, with the bike kicked off to the side—this is Ricky Carmichael doing the "whip."

Carmichael crashed early in the season and was injured. After that, he never finished higher than fourth in a race that season. Carmichael seemed to start getting the hang of things in 2000. He scored his first Supercross-class victory that year in Daytona, Florida, and in 2001, he put it all together, winning 13 races in a row. For the first time, Carmichael had dethroned "the King," Jeremy McGrath, and won his first Supercross championship.

The Hits Keep on Coming

Over the next 12 years, Carmichael won 46 events and five Supercross championships. He retired in 2007 with more than 140 victories in supercross and motocross combined. Although Carmichael no longer competes in SX, he's still into high-speed action. In 2006, he signed on to drive for the MB2 Motorsports NASCAR Nextel Cup team. Unfortunately, Carmichael was recently diagnosed with chronic fatigue syndrome—a disease that makes people feel exhausted. It is unclear how this might affect his future in NASCAR.

In the high speed, high-flying SX action, Carmichael flew higher than any other rider, winning seven Supercross championships.

Carmichael didn't look like a tough guy or a rough-and-tumble biker. His friendly, open face and his skills helped make him a fan favorite.

Here Comes Bubba

In the early 2000s, James "Bubba" Stewart was the next SX superstar to emerge. His skills and attitude made it seem like he could challenge even the records of McGrath and Carmichael.

On the Road

James Stewart Jr. has been called the "Tiger Woods of Supercross." Like Tiger Woods, Stewart got an early start in his sport. He was born on December 21, 1985, and it wasn't long before he found his way onto a bike. His father, James Sr., had raced in motocross and decided to teach his son about the sport that he loved. At age four, Stewart entered his first race. By the time he was seven, he already had his first **sponsor**! Also like Tiger Woods, Stewart comes from an African American family and has succeeded in a sport that has seen few black athletes.

Bubba Hits the Big Time

The Stewart family quickly recognized that their son had a special talent. They pulled James Jr. and his brother out of school and traveled to races around the country in a motor home. In between races and practice, Stewart and his brother were homeschooled. Stewart won a record 11 championships during his amateur career. (His family had nicknamed him "Boogie," but fans soon started calling him "Bubba" instead. It's not exactly clear where the name came from, but it stuck.) Stewart burst onto the supercross scene in 2002. He first raced in the Lites division, where he won four races in his first season (including the East-West Shootout), but narrowly lost the title to Californian Travis Preston. He kept at it, though, and in all, won a record 18 Lites events between 2002 and 2004. He also won championships in East Lites and West Lites.

No. 7 is lucky for this young superstar. Stewart aimed for the top spot from a young age, and he proved to have the skills and talent to make it.

Living the SX Dream

When Bubba was just 18, he was ready for the jump to the Supercross class, but he got off to a rocky start. In just the second race of the season, he broke his leg. After missing eight weeks of action, Stewart returned and won three of the remaining races. But by the end of 2005, Stewart's future was in doubt. He was battling mysterious stomach pains that turned out to be caused by an infection. After getting treatment, Stewart was as good as new. In 2006, he proved that he was ready to compete with the top riders in the world. He won eight events and finished in a tie for second for the Supercross Championship. The 2007 season was even more amazing for Stewart. He won 13 events and became the first African American to win a Supercross Championship. Just 22 years old going into 2008, Stewart had already scored 24 AMA Supercross class victories. Could he someday pass Carmichael's mark of 46 wins or challenge McGrath's all-time record of 72? Only time will tell, but with his combination of skill and determination, you wouldn't want to bet against Bubba.

The Lites class was Stewart's "coming-out party." His success at this lower-level SX racing primed him for a move to the big-time.

Bubba Stewart's dad James (right) has always been his son's biggest fan and the most important member of the Stewart racing team.

Top Supercross-Class Winners

Riders	Wins
Jeremy McGrath	72
Ricky Carmichael	46
Ricky Johnson	28
Bob Hannah	27
Chad Reed*	26
James Stewart, Jr.*	24

(Through 2007)
*Still active as of 2007.

The Biggest Show on Two Wheels

The motorcycles rev, the mud flies, riders shoot off jumps high into the sky! A supercross event is an exciting show whether you watch it on TV or grab a seat among thousands of screaming fans at a live event.

Top Tour Stops

Every year, the AMA Supercross series brings exciting events to fans across the country. The series kicks off in early January at Angel Stadium in Anaheim, California. This is the first of two AMA events held at Angel Stadium, which is why it's called Anaheim 1. It is considered the sport's biggest race. A total of 17 tour events are held at stadiums around the United States and Canada. One popular stop is Reliant Stadium in Houston, Texas, which has a retractable roof and more than 125,000 square feet of space for racing. The Georgia Dome in Atlanta, which has been holding races since 1977, draws 70,000 fans to its annual event.

Making Tracks

Before any supercross event can take place, there's lots of work to be done. To create the one-to two-mile (1.6-3.2 km) SX tracks, hundreds of tons of dirt must be hauled into the stadium. Special flooring is put down first to protect the turf and the stadium floor. Bulldozers and other equipment are then used to turn that dirt into a challenging course. When they're done, the tracks contain a variety of obstacles, such as "whoops" (a series of large bumps), and triple jumps, which can shoot riders 40 feet into the air! Safety and starting areas are created at different points, too. The trick is to make a track that is challenging, safe, and easy for fans to see.

Bulldozers and tractors move around tons of dirt on arena floors to create SX courses. They can do the job in just a few days.

Points and Prizes

The main attractions at each of the tour's events are the Supercross-class events. Riders compete in a series of qualifying races and then face off in a final race known as the "main event." The riders earn cash prizes based on where they finish. Riders also are awarded points toward the AMA Supercross Championship. The winner of a race receives 25 points, the second-place rider gets 22, the third-place rider gets 20, and so on. At the end of the season, the rider with the most points wins the AMA Supercross Class Championship. The standings can be so close that the last event in Las Vegas can decide the champion. Supercross-class races are not the only attraction at an SX event. The Lites division is also a big part of any Supercross event (see page 22). Many of the events also include laser light shows and other fun activities to entertain the fans.

Fireworks are part of the show at the AMA season-kickoff event in Anaheim.

This overhead view gives a good look at the twisting, turning route that riders must take around this course at Qualcomm Stadium in San Diego.

Don't worry, they turn off the laser light show at this event in Las Vegas before the riders take the course!

Under the Sky

The AMA Supercross series is an important part of supercross racing, but it's not the only game in town. With only 17 tour events each year, riders have plenty of time to explore other races. This allows them to get more experience, get more exposure, and, of course, earn more money. Many supercross riders race in outdoor motocross events. The AMA Motocross tour starts in May, after the AMA Supercross tour is over. This allows riders to participate in both without missing any key events.

Big One-Time Events

Individual "one-off" supercross events are also popular. That means they are not part of the regular schedule of AMA events, but are still important races to take part in. Some of these are held in the United States, while others are held overseas. The U.S. Open in Las Vegas is probably the biggest of these events. It has been held at the MGM Grand Garden Arena every year since 1998. The two-day event has featured both Lites and Supercross class races. They don't count toward the Supercross Championship, but they do offer riders other rewards. The top prize for the U.S. Open is $100,000, and riders can win up to $250,000 by winning a certain combination of races. That's a pretty good haul for a day or two on a motorcycle!

Crossing Over to Arenacross

Some supercross riders choose to cross over and try out the smaller tracks of arenacross. Top supercross riders Danny Smith, Chad Johnson, and Brock Sellards all competed in arenacross in 2007. Arenacross events take place over a two-day period. In 2007, there were two main Arenacross tours: the Toyota AMA Arenacross Series and the BooKoo Arenacross Championship. The Toyota series is approved by the AMA and included 19 events in 2007. BooKoo had 10 races in 2007, but it featured an exciting new event called the BooKoo U.S. Open of Arenacross. It was held at the 10,000-seat Mohegan Sun Arena in Uncasville, Connecticut. A nearly full house saw 15-year-old Tyler Bowers win the event. He took home the top prize of $50,000!

Tight quarters: Grant Langston (8) gets the inside edge around this curve during a supercross race. Riders can find themselves just inches away at high speed.

Two of the best: Jeremy McGrath (2) and Chad Reed (22) are shown high above the race course during a supercross event.

Lighting Up the Lites

Although the Supercross class is by the far the biggest draw in the sport, the Lites division is also a big hit with fans. Lites are not "lightweights"! In fact, the top Lites riders actually have faster lap times than most SX riders do.

Starting Out in the Lites

The Lites class was created in the 1980s. This class used to be considered a sort of minor league. Young riders would get their feet wet racing on less powerful bikes. They also faced a lower level of competition. After getting some experience, the best riders would then move up to the bigger bikes and the brighter lights. The Lites still serve this purpose today. Every supercross rider, even the greatest ones, starts out riding in the Lites. That makes the Lites a great place to spot up-and-coming talent. Fans checking out Lites races in the early 1990s would have gotten a sneak peak at future legend Jeremy McGrath. Just a few years ago, James Stewart Jr. could be spotted showing his stuff in the Lites division.

Lites Reach New Heights

Like every part of supercross, Lites has seen a recent boost in its popularity. It is now a big draw in its own right. Some fans (and riders) enjoy the more aggressive, all-out style that's possible on the smaller cycles. The class is also a chance for motorcycle makers to show off their smaller models. Ben Townley, Ryan Villopoto, and Josh Grant are fan favorites who starred in the Lites in 2007. The Lites also have their own championships. The class is broken down into

Another victory in the Lites class for top rider Ryan Villopoto. SX races end with a jump across the finish line.

The East-West Shootout brings together top riders from across the United States.

Lites East and Lites West divisions. Each of the first 15 stops on the AMA tour has a Lites competition that falls into one of these regions. At the end of the season, the points are tallied up and Supercross Lites East and Supercross Lites West champions are crowned. The last event of the AMA series is one of the most exciting in Lites competition. The top riders from each region come together at Sam Boyd Stadium in Las Vegas. They face off in one final race: the East/West Shootout. The race determines the top Lites racer in the United States! Interestingly, the winner of the East/West Shootout is almost never one of the Lites-class champions. In fact, the only time a champ has won the Shootout this century is when James Stewart Jr. did it in 2002.

Current SX star James Stewart Jr. began his rise to the top by winning the Lites championship and also winning the East-West Shootout.

Smooth Rides: The Bikes of Supercross

Supercross riders rely on one piece of equipment more than any other—their bikes. Let's take a look at these mean machines. Most are highly modified versions of the same bikes you can buy at your local motorcycle dealer.

How They Got Here

The bikes have come a long way since the early days of motocross. Early in the 20th century, motorcycles were pretty much just bicycles with small engines. By the 1970s, the bikes had stronger engines, but they were also big and bulky. Today's supercross riders use bikes that are more powerful, lighter, and easier to handle than bikes of the past. Many riders ride for motorcycle makers who provide them with a bike. Some riders are independent and have custom bikes made for them. But just about every rider has a team that helps keep his bike in top shape.

Ever-Changing Engines

Until recently, the SX racing classes were named for the engines of the bikes being used. Lites class was known as 125 class because it used 125cc machines. Supercross class was known as 250 because it used 250cc bikes. Those are measures of the size of the engine. A 250cc engine has a **cylinder** that is 250 cubic centimeters. A larger cylinder allows more gas to be burned and more power to be produced. In recent years, Supercross-class riders have moved to using 450cc bikes, and the Lites have moved up to 250cc machines. A key difference is that these new bikes have

The driver rides alone, but he has a big team of helpers behind him. Here's James Stewart Jr. with some of his dozen or so crew members.

four-stroke engines, rather than the two-stroke engines of the past. Four-stroke engines are more efficient, cleaner, and more durable. But they are not as powerful and are also heavier. So even though the 250cc bikes that are used in the Lites class today are more powerful than the 125cc machines of the past were, they are not twice as powerful.

A Rider's Support System

Supercross riders need a lot of help making sure that they and their bikes stay in top racing shape. A rider's team includes lots of helpers. The leader of the team is the manager, who is heavily involved in every aspect of racing, from equipment to training to strategy. Another important team member is the mechanic, also known as the "wrench." The wrench is in charge of making sure the bike is performing at its best.

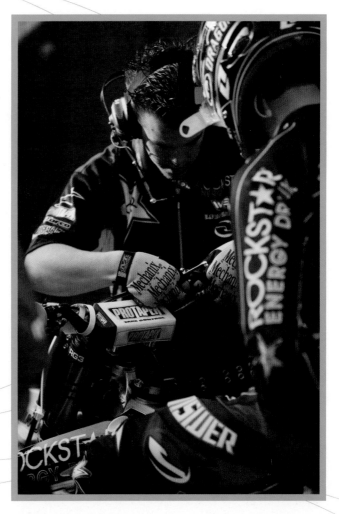

In the pit area, bikes are on display when they're not being worked on. The bikes are placed on small stands so they stay upright for viewing.

Ace mechanics are always ready to jump in to fix a broken bike or to make an adjustment that might gain the rider a bit more speed.

Tricks of the Trade

Supercross riders are serious about winning, but they also like to have fun. Performing tricks is one way for riders to get their kicks while entertaining the fans. Some riders have even given up racing to do tricks for a living!

SX Tricks

The whip and the Nac-Nac are the tricks that you're most likely to see at a supercross race. To do a whip, a rider pulls, or whips, his bike up and to the side when going over a jump. Some riders do this with such great force that their bike ends up completely sideways in the air. Jeremy McGrath introduced the Nac-Nac to supercross in 1994. To perform a Nac-Nac, the rider swings both legs to the same side of the bike while flying through the air.

Freestyling

Tricks used to be fairly common during supercross races, but they are less so today. These days, riders save many of their most exciting moves for what are known as freestyle motocross events. These started in the mid-1990s. The International Freestyle Motocross Association (IFMA) held its first events in 1998. Today, it holds more than 40 competitions each year. The action-sports-focused X Games added a freestyle motocross event to their schedule in 1999. It's been a big hit ever since.

Don't try this at home! Freestyle riders perform gravity-defying moves like this one, a heel-clicker flip, before thousands of cheering fans.

FMX Superstar

Travis Pastrana is probably the biggest star of freestyle riding. Travis is a successful supercross rider who won a Lites East championship in 2001. But he has found that he's best at thrilling crowds with his amazing moves. Travis has won several X Games gold medals. He landed the first ever double backflip during the 2006 X Games.

Travis's Tricks

Riders are always trying out new tricks or modifying old tricks. They love the chance to be creative on their bikes. But they are also concerned about safety. They practice their tricks for a long time before performing them. And they wear protective gear to avoid injury. Here are some slick tricks that you might see Travis Pastrana and other riders try in a freestyle event:

Cancan: The rider puts both legs on the same side of the bike, and kicks one out to the side, as if he's doing the old-fashioned cancan dance.

Heel-clicker: The rider brings both feet up over the bike's handlebars. He brings his legs around his arms and clicks his heels together.

Superman Seat Grab: The rider lets go of the handlebars and holds on to the seat instead. With his body stretched out behind the bike, he looks like Superman flying through the sky.

Travis Pastrana goes back in time to do a Nac-Nac (left) while getting in some practice on a sand dune. Ricky Carmichael shows off his high-flying style with a whip during an SX event.

The Next Generation: The Amateurs

Even superstars like McGrath, Carmichael, and Stewart had to start somewhere. The many top amateur events held in the U.S. prepare riders for the "big time." Some kids are lucky enough to race in a stadium filled with thousands of people.

The First Steps

All professional supercross riders start out riding in amateur motocross events. Young riders use smaller, less powerful bikes called minicycles. They race on outdoor courses in a variety of races and classes. Despite these differences from the indoor sport, amateur MX racing is still a great way to pick up the skills that are needed in supercross. The motocross amateur ranks are where almost all SX riders get their start. For example, Ricky Carmichael set the record for AMA amateur championships with 10. A few years later, James Stewart Jr. surpassed that mark with 11 championships.

The chance to be cheered by thousands and to run around on the dirt floor of an arena is a big part of the appeal of the KTM Junior Supercross events.

Top Amateur Events

Amateur motocross races are held around the country. One of the most well known series of races is Loretta Lynn's AMA Amateur Motocross National Championships. This consists of a series of races that are held in seven regions around the United States. Each region holds several area **qualifier** races. The top riders from each of those move on to the regional championships. The top riders at each of those races get to go to the Loretta Lynn Amateur National Championships at the country singer's track in Tennessee. The U.S. Open, one of the biggest events in motocross, also features an event for youngsters. The top-12 riders in the 85cc class of the Loretta Lynn event are invited to participate. The Amateur Arenacross World Finals, held on a slightly toned-down track the day after the U.S. Open, gives young riders a chance to compete on one of the biggest stages in the sport. Fans get to see riders who may someday be the top supercross and motocross riders.

Riders who take part in the Loretta Lynn events are singing a sweet tune, with the chance to strut their stuff against the best young riders.

Kids' Supercross

Most amateur events are for the outdoor MX riders, but there is a chance for kids to try supercross. The KTM Junior Supercross Challenge (KJSC) is held at 16 AMA SX races each year. Riders who are seven to eight years old are eligible to compete. Both boys and girls are welcome, but all riders must also be under 52 inches tall and weigh less than 70 pounds. They also must have experience riding, as well as have above-average grades in school. Between 150 and 180 riders apply to participate. The lucky few who get chosen are outfitted with riding gear and sent out onto the same course that the pros use. The races are a great chance for youngsters to get a first-hand look at the exciting world of SX.

Young riders who take part in the KTM Junior Supercross events get great exposure to big-time racing while still competing against kids their own age.

Down the Road with Supercross

Although it's hard to believe, supercross is still growing in popularity. By some estimates, it is now the second-biggest motor sport behind NASCAR. The sport is also branching out in several ways. Every day, new fans get turned on to supercross.

The Media Mob

One major contributor to the sport's growth has been the media. Some of the top races are broadcast on ESPN, Speed TV, and other networks. ESPN also organizes and broadcasts the X Games, which include popular freestyle motocross events. Riders, sponsors, the AMA, and others also maintain online Web sites. These give fans instant access to race results, interviews, photos, and other information. Magazines also help keep fans up to date on the latest news and the newest equipment. In 2005, a feature film was even made about supercross. *Supercross: The Movie* didn't do very well at the box office or with the critics, but it did allow many new fans to see the excitement of racing on the big screen. The *MX vs. ATV* video games series has proven to be a bigger hit with fans than the movie was. In these games, players get to control bikes of motocross riders (MX) or all-terrain vehicles (ATVs) while they navigate off-road courses.

The X Games' popularity has helped more and more fans see exciting motorcycle action in person and on TV.

Minibikes and More

There are more new draws to the sport beyond flicking on the TV or popping in a video game. The creation of "minibikes" has put a new twist on the sport. These cycles are much smaller and pack less of a punch. They are also more affordable, which has allowed many fans to try out riding on a small scale. Competitive minibike races, such as the Minimoto SX in Las Vegas, have become popular events. Jeremy McGrath and other supercross riders have tried their hands in these races. Perhaps the most important development of all is that supercross is reaching young fans. Whether they are competing on the amateur level, playing MX vs. ATV, or attending a live supercross event, kids are connecting with supercross. The speed, style, and excitement of supercross promises to keep kids and adults coming back for more.

James Stewart Jr. (7, center) waits for the gate to drop to start an SX race. The dirt-churning first few yards always make for racing excitement.

Giants riding SX bikes?! No, it's the bikes that are small. That's Jeremy McGrath (2) ready to hit the throttle on his Minimoto.

Glossary

agile   Nimble, quick, flexible

amateur   A person who does a sport or an activity without being paid

ATV   Short for a three- or four-wheel vehicle known as an all-terrain vehicle

BMX   Bicycle motocross, racing on dirt riding small bicycles

cylinder   The chamber in which a piston of an engine moves.

grassroots   Starting from the bottom or from among the people

import   Something imported, or brought in from another country.

media   People from TV, radio, newspapers, magazines, and Internet sites who report news

NASCAR   National Association for Stock Car Auto Racing

pit area   The part of a race track where vehicles are worked on and where drivers wait between events

promoter   A person who organizes, and often pays for, putting on a sports or entertainment event

qualifier   An event that helps decide which athletes will proceed to a higher-level event

sponsor   A person or a company that provides funds for an event in return for advertising time

tri-oval   A race track that resembles a triangle with rounded edges

Index

Printed in the U.S.A.